C L A S S I C
CHILDREN'S
STORIES

READER'S DIGEST YOUNG FAMILIES, INC.

Cover illustrated by Richard Bernal

Title page illustrated by Holly Jones

This edition is published by Reader's Digest Young Families, Inc.

Pleasantville, NY 10570

www.readersdigest.com

Reader's Digest Young Families is a trademark of The Reader's Digest Association, Inc.

Louis Weber, C.E.O.

Publications International, Ltd.

7373 North Cicero Avenue

Lincolnwood, Illinois 60712

www.pubint.com

Manufactured in China.

8 7 6 5 4 3 2 1

ISBN: 0-7853-4741-0

CONTENTS

Hiawatha

Written by Henry Wadsworth Longfellow
Illustrated by Holly Jones

By the shores of Gitche Gumee,

By the shining Big-Sea-Water,

Stood the wigwam of Nokomis,

Daughter of the Moon, Nokomis.

Dark behind it rose the forest,

Rose the black and gloomy pine-trees,

Rose the firs with cones upon them;

Bright before it beat the water,

Beat the clear and sunny water

Beat the shining Big-Sea-Water.

There the wrinkled, old Nokomis

Nursed the little Hiawatha,

Rocked him in his linden cradle,

Bedded soft in moss and rushes,

Safely bound with reindeer sinews;

Stilled his fretful wail by saying,

"Hush! the Naked Bear will hear thee!"

Lulled him into slumber, singing,

"Ewa-yea! my little owlet!

Who is this, that lights the wigwam?

With his great eyes lights the wigwam?

Ewa-yea! my little owlet!"

Many things Nokomis taught him

Of the stars that shine in heaven;

Showed him Ishkoodah, the comet,

Ishkoodah, with fiery tresses;

Showed the Death-Dance of the spirits,

Warriors with their plumes and war-clubs,

Flaring far away to Northward

In the frosty nights of Winter;

Showed the broad white road in heaven,

Pathway of the ghosts, the shadows.

Running straight across the heavens,

Crowded with the ghosts, the shadows.

At the door on Summer evenings

Sat the little Hiawatha;

Heard the whispering of the pine-trees,

Heard the lapping of the waters,

Sounds of music, words of wonder.

Saw the fire-fly, Wah-wah-taysee,

Flitting through the dusk of evening,

With the twinkle of its candle

Lighting up the brakes and bushes,

And he sang the song of children,

Sang the song Nokomis taught him:

"Wah-wah-taysee, little fire-fly,

Little, flitting, white-fire insect.

Little, dancing, white-fire creature,

Light me with your little candle,

Ere upon my bed I lay me,

Ere in sleep I close my eyelids!"

Saw the moon rise from the water

Rippling, rounding from the water,

Saw the flecks and shadows on it,

Whispered, "What is that, Nokomis?"

And the good Nokomis answered:

"Once a warrior, very angry,

Seized his grandmother, and threw her

Up into the sky at midnight;

Right against the moon he threw her;

'T is her body that you see there."

Saw the rainbow in the heaven,

In the eastern sky, the rainbow,

Whispered, "What is that, Nokomis?"

And the good Nokomis answered:

"'T is the heaven of flowers you see there;

All the wild-flowers of the forest,

All the lilies of the prairie,

When on earth they fade and perish,

Blossom in that heaven above us."

When he heard the owls at midnight,

Hooting, laughing in the forest,

"What is that?" he cried in terror:

"What is that," he said, "Nokomis?"

And the good Nokomis answered:

"That is but the owl and owlet,

Talking in their native language,

Talking, scolding at each other."

Then the little Hiawatha

Learned of every bird its language,

Learned their names and all their secrets,

How they built their nests in Summer

Where they hid themselves in Winter,

Talked with them whene'er he met them,

Called them "Hiawatha's Chickens."

Of all beasts he learned the language,

Learned their names and all their secrets,

How the beavers built their lodges,

Where the squirrels hid their acorns,

How the reindeer ran so swiftly,

Why the rabbit was so timid,

Talked with them whene'er he met them,

Called them "Hiawatha's Brothers."

George Washington and the Cherry Tree

Adapted by Catherine McCafferty
Illustrated by Jerry Harston

Many stories and books have been written about George Washington. When the American colonies fought for their freedom, Washington led the soldiers against the British. When the brand-new country needed a leader, Washington served as its first president.

The legend of George Washington's honesty is just as famous as these true stories of bravery. It is called a legend, because no one has any records to say that the story really happened. Did young George Washington chop down a cherry tree? Maybe not. But this story shows just how important it is for everyone to tell the truth.

What a fine day it was for young George Washington! At just six years old, he had his very own hatchet. George was proud of his new hatchet. It felt solid in his small hands. Its blade was shiny and sharp. George swung the hatchet through the air just to see the sun shine on it.

His father stopped him. "A hatchet is not a toy, George," his father warned. "It can do much harm if you are not careful. Always take care when you use it."

George nodded at his father's words. His father was talking to him like a man. Owning a hatchet was a serious thing, indeed. George promised he would always be very careful with it.

Once he was outside, though, George felt more excited than serious. His family's farm seemed full of things that needed cutting. George tested his hatchet on a row of weeds at the edge of the cornfield. It sliced through their thin stems. The row of tall weeds became a pile of cut weeds. George smiled as he was very pleased at the work he had done. He took aim at the thicker stalks of the corn plants.

Whack! Three cornstalks fell with a rustle and a crunch. George stepped back, startled. He looked at his hatchet with a new respect. His father was right. He would have to be careful. Then George saw that an ear of corn had fallen to the ground. It was even thicker than the cornstalks. George's hatchet sliced the corncob in half.

Not far from the cornfield, George's father tended to his fruit trees. He was proud of the sweet apples, peaches, and pears that the trees gave his family. He kept the trees' branches trimmed, and watched them for any sign of sickness. Mr. Washington gave extra attention to his youngest tree. It was a cherry tree, and it had come from far away. The cherry tree had been just a sapling when Mr. Washington planted it. Each year, Mr. Washington watched it grow stronger. This year, there were blossoms on its branches. Perhaps, he thought, it might even give fruit. Mr. Washington thought of the fresh cherries they could pick. Then he thought of the cherry pies Mrs. Washington could bake with the sweet cherries. He smiled and gave the cherry tree a pat.

George ran up to Mr. Washington as he walked back to the house for supper. "This hatchet works well, Father," he said.

His father smiled. "Yes, I've seen you using it."

When they sat down for dinner, George laid his hatchet down in a corner of the room. All through dinner, he looked over at it. What could he do with it next?

George thought about going into the woods and chopping down tree after tree. Then he thought about chopping the fallen trees into smaller pieces to be used in the fire to warm their home during the winter. "I would be so useful," George thought.

George's mother noticed how George watched the hatchet. "I think it's time you put that hatchet to good use, George," she said. "Tomorrow, I would like you to chop up kindling for the fire."

"Oh yes, Mother!" George said. "I can start tonight! I'll chop us enough kindling to last all winter long."

Mrs. Washington shook her head. "You'll do better work after a good night's sleep."

George put his hatchet under his bed. He climbed into bed and closed his eyes. After a few minutes, he leaned over the side of the bed and peeked at the floor. The hatchet was still there. George had a hard time falling asleep. He couldn't wait until morning. He saw himself chopping piles, and then mounds, and then mountains of kindling! Why, he would chop enough kindling to keep the kitchen fires burning for years! When George finally fell asleep, he dreamed that he was a great woodcutter. With one sweep of his hatchet, he cut down whole forests.

The next morning, George hurried through his breakfast. As soon as he finished his last bite, he told his mother, "I'm ready to chop kindling now." His mother sent him outside to the woodshed. George looked around for the kindling. It was not a mountain of kindling. And it was barely a mound. Still, George went to work. He chopped the long, thin branches into small sticks.

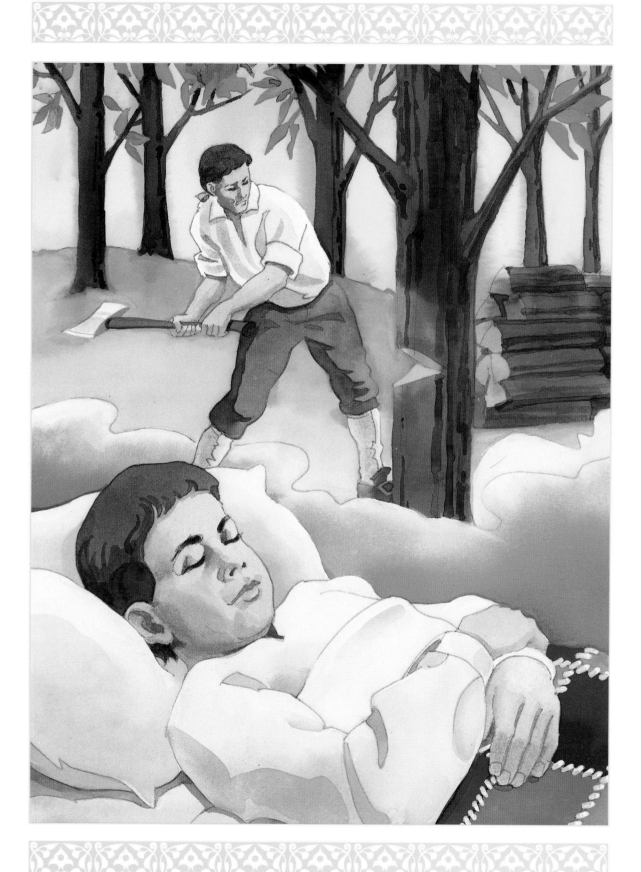

Then George chopped the small sticks into smaller sticks. Then he chopped the smaller sticks into pieces. George saw that the pieces were too small to be chopped further. He ran inside to tell his mother that he had finished his job.

"Is there any more kindling for me to chop, Mother?" George asked.

"No, George. You may play for a while," she said.

George didn't want to play. He wanted to use his hatchet. He thought of the cornstalks and the corncob he had cut yesterday. Then he tried to think of something else to cut.

"Mother," he said, "would you like me to chop some logs for the fire?"

Mrs. Washington smiled. "No, George. Those logs would be much too big for your hatchet to cut."

George wandered outside. Just how much could his hatchet cut? The kindling had been easy. It was so thin. The cornstalks and the corncob were thicker, but they had been easy to cut, too. George decided to test his hatchet again.

He went to an old, thick fence post. On the first strike, his hatchet's blade sunk deep into the wood. George had to tug to pull it free. "Well, that was too thick," George thought. George looked around for something thicker than the cornstalks but thinner than the fence post. Then he spotted the trunk of the young cherry tree.

The tree trunk looked just right. It wasn't full-grown as the apple and pear trees were. George chopped at the cherry tree. The blade dug into the tree trunk, but pulled free easily. Why, it would take just a few strokes of his hatchet to cut the tree down! George chopped until the tree fell. George looked proudly at the fallen tree. Then he remembered how much his father liked the cherry tree. And he remembered how his father had told him to be careful with the hatchet.

George hurried back to the woodshed. He sat in a dark corner. "Oh, what have I done?" George said to himself. "If only I had been careful, as father had told me."

Mr. Washington saw the fallen tree on his way to the house. He saw that its trunk was cut through with many strokes. Then he realized there would be no cherries. There would be no cherry pies. After all his hard work and care, there would be no cherry tree. George's father sadly walked back to the house.

George saw his father go past the woodshed. Slowly, he followed his father into the house. He carried the hatchet with him. George knew he had done a very bad thing.

His father turned as he heard George come in the door. He looked at George. He looked at George's hatchet. George could see that his father was very angry.

"George," his father said, "do you know who killed my cherry tree?"

George took a deep breath. His stomach knotted as he looked at his father. He tried not to think about how he would be punished. Instead George said, "I cannot tell a lie, Father. I cut down your cherry tree." George looked at his feet. He felt like crying, but he said, "I wasn't careful with the hatchet. I'm sorry, Father." Then he waited to hear what his punishment would be.

George felt his father's hands on his shoulders. "Look at me, Son," said Mr. Washington. George made himself look up at his father. To George's surprise, his father no longer seemed angry. In fact, Mr. Washington looked rather calm.

"You have been honest, Son," said Mr. Washington. "That means more to me than any cherry tree ever could."

Of course, George's father was disappointed that there would be no cherries to make cherry pies, but he also wanted to reward his son for telling the truth. George did something terribly wrong, but he wasn't punished, because he also did something right.

"So remember, no matter what the circumstance, you must always tell the truth," George's father added and proudly put his arm around his young son.

George never forgot his father's words. They were a lesson for life.

Paul Revere's Ride

Written by Henry Wadsworth Longfellow
Illustrated by Jon Goodell

Listen, my children, and you shall hear

Of the midnight ride of Paul Revere,

On the eighteenth of April, in Seventy-five,

Hardly a man is now alive

Who remembers that famous day and year.

He said to his friend, "If the British march

By land or sea from the town to-night,

Hang a lantern aloft in the belfry arch

Of the North Church tower as a signal light,

One, if by land, and two, if by sea;

And I on the opposite shore will be,

Ready to ride and spread the alarm

Through every Middlesex village and farm,

For the country folk to be up and to arm."

Then he said, "Good night!" and with muffled oar

Silently rowed to the Charlestown shore,

Just as the moon rose over the bay,

Where swinging wide at her moorings lay

The *Somerset*, British man-of-war;

A phantom ship, with each mast and spar

Across the moon like a prison bar,

And a huge black hulk, that was magnified

By its own reflection in the tide.

Meanwhile, his friend, through alley and street,

Wanders and watches with eager ears,

Till in silence around him he hears

The muster of men at the barrack door,

The sound of arms, and the tramp of feet,

And the measured tread of the grenadiers,

Marching down to their boats on the shore.

Then he climbed to the tower of the Old North Church,

By the wooden stairs, with stealthy tread,

To the belfry-chamber overhead,

And startled the pigeons from their perch

On the sombre rafters, that round him made

Masses and moving shapes of shade—

Up the trembling ladder, steep and tall,

To the highest window in the wall,

Where he paused to listen and look down

A moment on the roofs of the town,

And the moonlight flowing over all.

Beneath, in the churchyard, lay the dead,

In their night-encampment on the hill,

Wrapped in silence so deep and still

That he could hear, like a sentinel's tread,

The watchful night-wind, as it went

Creeping along from tent to tent,

And seeming to whisper, "All is well!"

A moment only he feels the spell

Of the place and the hour, and the secret dread

Of the lonely belfry and the dead;

For suddenly all his thoughts are bent

On a shadowy something far away,

Where the river widens to meet the bay,

A line of black that bends and floats

On the rising tide, like a bridge of boats.

Meanwhile, impatient to mount and ride,

Booted and spurred, with a heavy stride

On the opposite shore walked Paul Revere.

Now he patted his horse's side,

Now gazed at the landscape far and near,

Then, impetuous, stamped the earth,

And turned and tightened his saddle girth;

But mostly he watched with eager search

The belfry-tower of the Old North Church,

As it rose above the graves on the hill,

Lonely and spectral and sombre and still,

And lo! as he looks, on the belfry's height

A glimmer, and then a gleam of light!

He springs to the saddle, the bridle he turns,

But lingers and gazes, till full on his sight

A second lamp in the belfry burns!

A hurry of hoofs in a village street,

A shape in the moonlight, a bulk in the dark,

And beneath, from the pebbles, in passing, a spark

Struck out by a steed flying fearless and fleet;

That was all! And yet, through the gloom and the light,

The fate of a nation was riding that night;

And the spark struck out by that steed, in his flight,

Kindled the land into flame with its heat.

It was twelve by the village clock,

When he crossed the bridge into Medford town.

He heard the crowing of the cock,

And the barking of the farmer's dog,

And felt the damp of the river fog,

That rises after the sun goes down.

It was one by the village clock,

When he galloped into Lexington.

He saw the gilded weathercock

Swim in the moonlight as he passed,

And the meeting-house windows, blank and bare,

Gaze at him with a spectral glare,

As if they already stood aghast

At the bloody work they would look upon.

It was two by the village clock,

When he came to the bridge in Concord town.

He heard the bleating of the flock,

And the twitter of birds among the trees,

And felt the breath of the morning breeze

Blowing over the meadows brown.

And one was safe and asleep in his bed

Who at the bridge would be first to fall,

Who that day would be lying dead,

Pierced by a British musket ball.

You know the rest. In the books you have read,

How the British Regulars fired and fled,

How the farmers gave them ball for ball,

From behind each fence and farmyard wall,

Chasing the redcoats down the lane,

Then crossing the fields to emerge again

Under the trees at the turn of the road,

And only pausing to fire and load.

So through the night rode Paul Revere;

And so through the night went his cry of alarm

To every Middlesex village and farm,

A cry of defiance and not of fear,

A voice in the darkness, a knock at the door,

And a word that shall echo forevermore!

For, borne on the night-wind of the Past,

Through all our history, to the last,

In the hour of darkness and peril and need,

The people will waken and listen to hear

The hurrying hoofbeats of that steed,

And the midnight message of Paul Revere.

Rip Van Winkle

Adapted by Pegeen Hopkins
Illustrated by John Lund

If the legends of old are true, there is a touch of magic in the Catskill Mountains. They are the tall and beautiful cliffs that rise up far from the Hudson River. They reach so high that they nearly scrape the sky. If you look real close, on a clear day, you can see trails of smoke rising. The smoke comes from a sleepy, little town sitting at the base of the mysterious hills. This village was first settled by Dutchmen, in the oldest times, when the country was still very young. Many years ago, a simple, friendly man lived in that very town. His name was Rip Van Winkle.

Rip was a kind neighbor, loved by nearly everyone in town. When he walked through the streets, packs of children followed in his steps. They would ask for piggyback rides. Rip always agreed. He played games with them too, flew kites and shot marbles with them. Even the neighborhood dogs loved him. They never barked when Rip passed by.

Rip Van Winkle's only fault was that he hated work. It is not that he avoided any kind of moving around. He liked to go fishing in a stream. He would walk for hours hunting squirrels with his dog, Wolf. And Rip would never turn down a neighbor who asked for help.

But at home, Rip Van Winkle could do nothing right. His fences were always falling down. Weeds grew faster in his yard than anywhere else. And if his cow wasn't running away, she was ruining the fields.

His children were just as raggedy as his farm. They ran around wild, in ripped clothes. His son, Rip, was worst of all.

"That young Rip," everyone would say, "is going to turn out just like his father."

One autumn afternoon, Rip and Wolf wandered to the top of one of the highest mountains, by mistake. Late in the day, Rip threw himself down on the ground and enjoyed the beautiful countryside.

Just when Rip prepared to pick himself up and start home, he heard someone call his name. He turned and saw no one. Then he started down the hill. "Rip Van Winkle," he heard once more. Wolf began to growl. The fur on the back of his neck stood on end.

Rip looked around again. This time, his eyes fell on a strange little man, climbing up the hill. On his shoulder, the man carried a huge barrel almost bigger than himself.

"Would you mind helping me with this?" the little man asked.

"Of course," Rip replied. The man made Rip nervous, but he would never say no when asked for help.

Rip and the man walked up a small hill, while Wolf followed. As they made their way up, Rip heard loud claps and crashes. It sounded just like thunder. It seemed to come from the direction they were headed. Rip checked the sky. It still looked clear and blue.

"There must be a thunder shower on the other side of the mountain," Rip guessed. In fact, sudden rain showers were quite common this high in the mountains.

Passing through a deep crack in the mountain, they entered into a round clearing of grass. Mountains rose up on all sides. Once inside, Rip saw something very strange. On a flat spot in the center, there stood a crowd of little men. What a strange group they were.

What these men were doing was even more strange. Rip rubbed his eyes. The little men were bowling! They were throwing a ball at nine wooden pins that were sitting on the grass. No one made a noise. But every time the tiny ball rolled along the ground, the sound of thunder broke out.

When Rip and the little man reached the group, the men turned and stared at him.

One tiny man took the barrel from Rip's hand. He poured a thick, dark liquid from it into small mugs. Rip's companions motioned for him to take a mug for himself. Rip did. And he drank more than one glass.

Once Rip had finished several glasses, he felt tired. His eyes drooped, his vision blurred, and he drifted off into a deep sleep.

When Rip finally opened his eyes, it was morning. The sun shone high in the sky. Rip was lying with his head resting on a tree, right where he'd been when he first met the little man.

"Have I been asleep here all night?" Rip exclaimed in a panic. "Mrs. Van Winkle is going to be so angry! What am I going to tell her?"

Rip whistled for Wolf. The dog did not come running. "Maybe that little man ran off with my dog," Rip said. "Or maybe Wolf went home. I had better get there, too."

As he stood up, Rip's knees cracked. His legs hurt, as if he had not used them in a while. "Sleeping outside can't be good for me," Rip thought. His stomach growled. He was hungry for breakfast. When Rip started off down the hill, he was sad and a little confused.

As Rip got close to his village, he ran into a number of people. He did not know any of them. They were dressed strangely, too. He looked at them in surprise and saw looks of surprise on their faces as well. Something strange had happened, Rip thought.

After some odd looks, Rip finally looked down to see what everyone was staring at. His once clean-shaven face was now a long beard flowing down to his belly!

In town, a group of children raced after Rip, yelling and hollering. None of them looked familiar. Their dogs ran after him, barking and biting at Rip's heels. They did not know him, and he did not know them. Even the town itself looked different.

Rip passed streets full of houses that were not there before. His favorite places to visit were gone. Strange names appeared above the doors. He saw faces he did not know looking out at him from the windows.

Rip began to worry. He wondered if he and the entire town had fallen under some horrible spell. This had to be his hometown, the one he had left just the afternoon before. He looked over his shoulder. There, he saw the Catskill Mountains, the same as they had always been.

"I better head home," Rip said. "Things will surely be all right once I see Mrs. Van Winkle and the children."

After lots of searching and scratching his head, Rip was able to find his farm and his farmhouse. The house didn't look at all like he remembered it looking. The fence had fallen down completely, and the roof had partly fallen in. And there wasn't a soul in sight. Rip looked around the farm for some kind of movement.

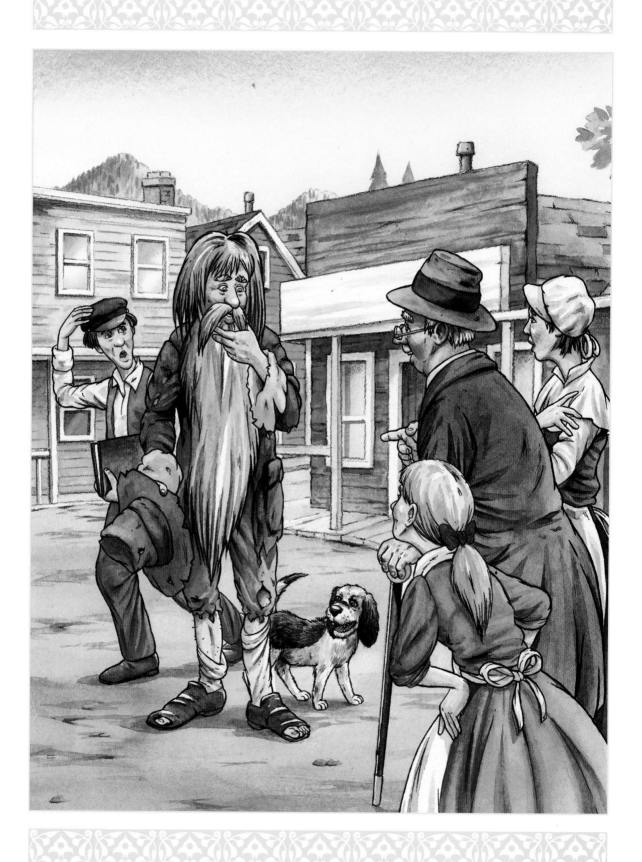

Rip walked up to the house slowly. With each step Rip became more and more afraid. The front door was swinging in the breeze.

Rip stepped inside the house. It was dark, and dust covered every inch of the space. It looked as though no one had lived in the house for many years. Time and neglect had ravaged Rip's house.

Rip ran to the center of town, looking for something familiar. His friends at the inn would have to know him. The building was gone though. In its place stood a tall pole topped with a red and white striped cloth waving in the wind. Then a group of men walked up to Rip.

"What are you doing here?" a tall man asked Rip. "Are you a Federalist or a Democrat? Did you fight in the Revolution?"

Rip had no idea what the man was talking about. Rip asked them, "Does anybody here know Rip Van Winkle?"

"Oh, sure," several of them answered. "That's Rip Van Winkle there, standing against that tree." Rip followed their pointed fingers. He saw someone that looked exactly like his old lazy self. The tall man walked up to Rip. He looked him in the eye and asked, "And just who exactly are you?"

"I was myself last night," Rip said. "I fell asleep on the mountain. Now everything has changed."

Right then a young woman with a baby in her arms pushed her way out of the crowd. She wanted to get a look at this old, gray-bearded man.

"What is your name, Miss?" Rip asked gently.

"Judith Gardenier," she replied.

"And your father's name?" Rip asked.

"Oh, Rip Van Winkle was his name. It's been twenty years since he took off into the mountains. His dog came home without him. We have heard nothing about him since. I was just a little girl then," the woman answered.

"And what about your mother?" Rip asked.

"She just recently died," the woman answered.

Hearing this, Rip could no longer contain himself. "I am your father," he cried and hugged her. "Once I was young Rip Van Winkle. Now I am old Rip Van Winkle. Doesn't anyone here know me?"

An old woman walked right up to Rip in the center of the crowd. She put her face almost to his, so she could see clearly. "Sure enough," she said. "Welcome home, Rip Van Winkle. Where have you been all these years?"

It did not take Rip long to tell his story. For him, all the years had passed in just one short night. The townspeople listened with wide eyes and amazement. But some people did not believe Rip Van Winkle. They insisted he was crazy.

The old Dutchmen, however, all believed him. To this day, whenever thunder crackles in the Catskills, they say it is the gnomes playing their strange lawn game. Who knows, it just may be true.

Paul Bunyan

Adapted by Jennifer Boudart
Illustrated by Gino D'Achille

An amazing baby was once born in the state of Maine. Paul Bunyan was like no other baby seen before or since. When he was only two weeks old, he weighed more than 100 pounds! He ate five dozen eggs, ten sacks of potatoes, and a barrel of oatmeal each day, just for breakfast!

Paul's parents loved him very much. They didn't mind paying expensive food bills or ordering custom-made booties in size 200. The real trouble started when Paul was only a year old and he started to crawl. Do you know what happens when a 500-pound baby crawls around? Earthquakes, that's what! The whole town shook with them!

The townspeople rushed to their crumbling town hall and took a vote. The mayor delivered the news to Paul's parents, "We're sorry, but you'll have to take Paul away."

The Bunyans reluctantly hauled their son to a cave deep in the woods. "We'll miss you, Paul," cried Mrs. Bunyan. "But we can't keep you at home. You're just too big!"

Mr. Bunyan handed Paul an ax, a knife, a fishing pole, and some flint rocks to make a fire. "You'll need these, Son," he said and patted Paul's giant knee.

"Good-bye," they said and walked away.

That night, Paul felt scared and lonely for the first time. He was so lonely that he cried giant tears for a month. Soon his giant tears turned into a great river! And he might have drowned himself in his tears if he hadn't heard a flop, flop, flop!

When Paul looked down, he saw a fish jumping in his river of tears. He caught it with his father's fishing pole, he cleaned it with his father's knife, and he cooked it over a fire made with his father's flint stones. Then Paul enjoyed his fish dinner and smiled for the first time in a month.

Paul Bunyan lived in his cave for the next 20 years. He lived off the land, he worked hard, and he grew to have the strength of 50 men.

When Paul awoke on his 21st birthday, he knew something was different. He looked outside his cave to see gusts of blue snow blowing and swirling past him! Paul pulled on his warmest clothes and ran outside to see what it was.

The snow felt cold upon his face. He held out his tongue and tasted the cold, blue snowflakes. Then Paul heard a sound over the wind: "Maa-maa, maa-maa." It sounded like a baby!

Paul rushed through the woods. "Where are you, baby?" he shouted. Suddenly he spotted a blue tail under a giant snowdrift. He pulled on the tail and out came the biggest ox on earth! Except for its white horns, the animal was frozen blue as the snow.

"Maa-maa," rumbled the giant, blue ox. "There, there, Babe," whispered the giant, bearded man. Paul took the ox back to his cave and built a blazing fire. He fell asleep with his arm around the ox and a wish on his lips: "Please, let Babe live."

Sure enough, the very next morning, Paul awoke to an enormous blue tongue licking his face. Babe had thawed out and warmed up! "You're alive!" Paul exclaimed as he hugged the mighty ox. He was so happy to see his new friend.

From that day forward, Paul Bunyan and Babe the Blue Ox were the best of friends. They went everywhere together, and the earth shook with each footstep they took.

Babe grew quick as blue lightning. Paul liked to close his eyes for ten seconds and then see how much Babe had grown. When Babe was finally full-grown, his horns towered over the treetops.

But that blue ox was just as gentle as he was big. He would do anything for his friend Paul.

Paul loved the deep, dark forests around his cave. Paul also knew how much people needed the trees that grew there. They used the wood from the trees to build new houses, churches, ships, and barns. So one day, Paul turned to Babe and said, "Friend, we have some work to do."

Paul gave his ax a mighty swing as he turned in a circle. "Tim-ber!" he yelled. One after another, ten trees fell to the ground: thump, thump, thump, thump, thump, thump, thump, thump, thump, thump . . . THUMP! "Let's float these trees downriver to the sawmill," said Paul. He piled the trees on Babe's strong back, and the friends set off for the Big Onion River.

Since Paul and Babe could cover a whole mile in one step, it took them only a week to travel from Maine to the Big Onion River in Minnesota. Then they floated the logs to a sawmill. That's when Paul decided being a lumberjack was the life for him. He and Babe would travel around the country cutting down trees.

Paul and Babe turned every head when they showed up for their first day of work at a new logging camp. No one had ever seen such a big man or ox before. Of course, Paul wasn't used to seeing people at all. They were so small compared to Paul. So at first, Paul made some mistakes.

When Paul had a terrible cold, he kept working and just used a bedsheet for a handkerchief. "AH-CHOO!" Paul sneezed a terrible sneeze the size of a hurricane, and he forgot to cover his mouth! The loggers grabbed onto tree trunks as they flew through the air.

"Cover your mouth," they yelled, "or we'll end up in China!"

Paul learned quickly, though. He stopped trying to shake hands, he didn't raise his voice above a whisper, and he always watched where he stepped.

Soon, Paul Bunyan and Babe the Blue Ox became the most famous lumberjack team in the land. Wherever they went, trees fell like twigs in the wind. They helped out in other ways, too. Lumberjacks were always trading stories about Paul's good deeds.

"Paul Bunyan went fishing with his bare hands! He grabbed enough fish to keep us fed for weeks!" said the cook.

"Paul Bunyan's ox made us a swimming pool with one scrape of his hoof," said the head lumberjack.

"Paul Bunyan cleared my whole yard of leaves with one breath," said the minister's wife.

Paul's new friends did nice things for him and Babe, too. They made Paul a belt from wagon wheels and rope. They gave him a pine-tree comb. They even sewed tents into booties to keep Babe's feet warm during the long winter.

Things went well until the spring of the Great Floods. "The rains are rising up from the ground instead of falling down from the sky!" Paul told Babe. "The other lumberjacks can't get to the trees to do their choppin'!"

Luckily, Paul wasn't just big on heart. He was big on brains, too. After thinking for a moment, Paul knew just what to do. "Order two thousand umbrellas," shouted Paul.

When the train dropped off the umbrellas, Paul cut off their handles. He showed the crew how to strap the umbrellas onto their feet. The crew floated across the flooded camp and right into the forest. "Ya-hoo!" the men cheered. But Paul would have another problem to solve soon.

The Great Floods also brought a swarm of ten-foot bees. They buzzed throughout the camp, stinging the men. The loggers couldn't leave their bunkhouses to work. Paul ordered a sugar boat to sail up the river. The bees swooped down and followed that sugar boat. They ate so much sugar, they couldn't fly off the deck. The boat sailed away and took the bees to a circus.

"Ya-hoo!" the men cheered again. Paul saved the day!

Paul and Babe floated logs downriver for many years. Each evening Paul took a walk with Babe. They would look out over the land and give thanks for their good fortune. The lumber company is gone, now. What about Paul and Babe? The next time you're in the woods, stop and listen. Maybe you'll hear the far-off sound of "Tim-ber!" on the wind.

THE
END